My Blanket is Blue

For Reuben – and for his sisters,
Leonie and Emilia

A Red Fox Book

Published by Random House Children's Books
20 Vauxhall Bridge Road, London SW1V 2SA
A division of The Random House Group Ltd
London Melbourne Sydney Auckland
Johannesburg and agencies throughout the world

Copyright © Hilda Offen 1998

1 3 5 7 9 10 8 6 4 2

First published in Great Britain by Hutchinson Children's Books 1998
Red Fox edition 2000

Printed in Singapore by Tien Wah Press (PTE) Ltd

THE RANDOM HOUSE GROUP Limited Reg. No. 954009
www.randomhouse.co.uk

ISBN 0 09 940873 2

My Blanket is Blue

Sleeptime ★ Dreamtime

Hilda Offen

RED
FOX

(WHISPER) *My blanket is soft,*
My blanket is blue.

When Mum says, 'Sleep tight',
Do you know what I do?

I say to my friends,
'Are you ready to go?
Let's fly to the North
And play in the snow!'

With the moon to our left
And the stars to our right,
We fly through the sky –
We fly through the night!

My blanket is cuddly –

It's warmer than toast.

I can scare off the bears.
'Shoo, Bears! I'm a ghost!'

(WHISPER) *My blanket is soft,*
My blanket is blue.

'Let's go,' says the cat.
'It's too cold for me!'

So we fly to the South
And swim in the sea.

I can lie in my hammock

Or sit in the shade.

I can play Bouncing Bears
And drink lemonade.

(WHISPER) *My blanket is soft,*
My blanket is blue.

I can stand on my head,

Ask a tiger to tea,

Tuck him up if he's ill.

So – Three Cheers for me!

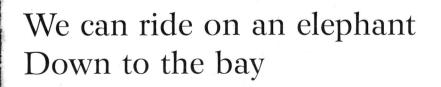

We can ride on an elephant
Down to the bay

Where my boat will be waiting
To take us away.

We sail on the sea,
We sail through the night –

All the way to my room
Where Mum says, 'Sleep tight!'

My friends sigh and yawn;
They snuggle down, too.

(WHISPER) *My blanket is soft,*
My blanket is blue.

Some bestselling Red Fox picture books

THE BIG ALFIE AND ANNIE ROSE STORYBOOK
by Shirley Hughes
OLD BEAR
by Jane Hissey
OI! GET OFF OUR TRAIN
by John Burningham
DON'T DO THAT!
by Tony Ross
NOT NOW, BERNARD
by David McKee
ALL JOIN IN
by Quentin Blake
THE WHALES' SONG
by Gary Blythe and Dyan Sheldon
JESUS' CHRISTMAS PARTY
by Nicholas Allan
THE PATCHWORK CAT
by Nicola Bayley and William Mayne
WILLY AND HUGH
by Anthony Browne
THE WINTER HEDGEHOG
by Ann and Reg Cartwright
A DARK, DARK TALE
by Ruth Brown
HARRY, THE DIRTY DOG
by Gene Zion and Margaret Bloy Graham
DR XARGLE'S BOOK OF EARTHLETS
by Jeanne Willis and Tony Ross
WHERE'S THE BABY?
by Pat Hutchins